THE
CARAVANSERAI
STORIES

TAHIR SHAH

THE
CARAVANSERAI
STORIES

TAHIR SHAH

MMXXI

Secretum Mundi Publishing Ltd
Kemp House
City Road
London
EC1V 2NX
United Kingdom

www.secretum-mundi.com
info@secretum-mundi.com

First published by Secretum Mundi Publishing Ltd, 2021
VERSION 13092021

THE CARAVANSERAI STORIES

© TAHIR SHAH

Tahir Shah asserts the right to be identified as the Author of the Work
in accordance with the Copyright, Designs and Patents Act 1988.
A CIP catalogue record for this title is available from the British Library.

The artwork for all the stories is drawn from the archive of The Rijks
Museum, Amsterdam — except for the illustrations for Ghoul Brothers,
which was drawn by Anca Chelaru.

Visit the author's website at:

Tahirshah.com

ISBN 978-1-912383-93-1

CONTENTS

GHOUL BROTHERS

*Eight strangers were clustered
around the campfire
of the caravanserai —
silhouetted, ragged, and
ripened by adventure.
As the flames licked
the darkness, sparks
spitting up into the desert's
nocturnal firmament,
the traveller dressed in
indigo cleared his throat
and told his tale:*

THE SIXTH SON of the sixth son, I was raised in a family blessed with good health and fine fortune.

My brothers and I had splendid clothing to wear, delicious food to eat, and were educated by private tutors. There was, however, a certain misfortune of which no one ever spoke.

Unlike me, or our parents, all five of my brothers were ghouls.

As I had never known siblings any different, I was happy enough with the ones I had. It was only as I grew from infancy into adolescence that I came to see they were unusual.

In day-to-day life, something else stood out about them more than the fact they were ghouls. You see, each one was deficient in one of the five senses.

The oldest, Gorem, was blind.

The next, Sorem, was deaf.

Then there was Korem, who had no sense of smell.

After him came Porem, who couldn't feel.

And lastly, Dorem, whose mouth didn't taste.

Being the youngest, I would play tricks on them all — delighting in the mischief I caused. Despite me causing trouble for them all, each one appeared to love me.

On the night of the brightest harvest moon I can remember, my ghoul brothers lined up in the great hall of our family home. One by one they announced they'd fallen in love.

Our parents were effusive with their congratulations and asked whether the brides-to-be had accepted.

'I have not asked her yet,' said Gorem.

'Neither have I,' said Sorem.

'Nor I,' said Korem.

'Me neither,' said Porem.

'Nor I,' said Dorem.

Our father stepped forwards and cleared his throat.

'Well, at least tell me the names of the lucky women,' he said.

'Her name is Amberine,' said Gorem.

'Her name is Amberine,' said Sorem.

'Her name is Amberine,' said Korem.

'Her name is Amberine,' said Porem.

'Her name is Amberine,' said Dorem.

Stepping forwards, our mother let out a shriek.

'Surely, each of the five brides-to-be are not named Amberine?!' she exclaimed.

With a sigh, I stepped forwards.

'Dearest mother and father,' I said, 'all five of them have fallen in love with the same girl.'

Our parents conferred for a good long time. Then, both at once, they asked:

'And what of Amberine — whom does she love?'

The ghoul brothers flinched.

'We don't know,' they said in time with one another.

Again, our parents conferred. When they'd discussed the matter long and hard, our father turned to me:

'Go to Amberine,' he said, 'and enquire gently whether she might grace us with her presence.'

The next evening, the potential bride ventured to our home, her brother as chaperone. The fact that all five of my ghoul brothers were in love with her was explained by my father. And the fact that she was not expected to even like any of them was explained by my mother.

A glint in her eye, Amberine stepped forwards to where all five of my siblings were lined up in order of age.

'I will marry the one who brings me the object of my dreams.'

'What is the object of your dreams?' the brothers asked.

'It's the one thing that touches all the senses,' she said.

The information was relayed to Sorem in sign language, while the others wondered aloud what such an object could be.

One by one, my ghoul brothers vowed not to return without the object of Amberine's dreams, and left on their adventures.

I went to bed in the most silent house in existence. Never once, through a long and crowded childhood, had I imagined our home could be so quiet as it was on that night.

When morning eventually came, I found my parents sitting on the balcony.

My mother rolled her eyes.

'Oh, what young men will do for the want of a woman,' she said.

'I wonder which of them shall win her hand,' my father added.

'I think I know the answer,' I said.

A week slipped by, in which the house seemed quieter with every minute that passed.

Then, a month came and went.

And before we knew it, an entire year had elapsed.

As the full moon rose up over the fields, the silhouettes of five figures were spotted streaming in from all directions of the compass.

Running to the window, I watched as they entered one by one.

First came Gorem.

After him, Sorem.

Korem was next.

Then Porem.

And close behind was Dorem.

While they rested, a message was sent to Amberine.

She arrived at noon the next day, her brother as chaperone once again.

On one side of the hall, Amberine, her brother, my parents, and I took places on low divans.

Across from us, my five ghoul brothers stood to attention.

When invited to do so, each one told the tale of his journey, before revealing what he imagined to be the object of Amberine's dreams.

As ever, Gorem went first:

'I may be blind, but my inability to see is the reason I'll win the hand of my lovely bride-to-be,' he said. 'Unlike my brothers standing beside me, I am not hindered by the follies besetting those born with sight. As such, I was able to hone my other senses on the adventure, and to perceive the true nature of the quest.

'I travelled east, along the snaking river, through a succession of dominions and kingdoms. Guided by the kindness of strangers and by a burning zeal to succeed, I followed a long, twisting trail of clues.

'For weeks and months I wandered, until at last I came to a forest as thick as any other in the Kingdom of Unfortunate Salvation. An informant there had revealed that a jinn, residing in the trees, could answer any question posed by a troubled mind.

'And he was right. For, as I was to discover, the most terrible creature imaginable existed there. He would surely have devoured me. But, thinking fast, I begged forgiveness for trespassing, and recounted to him the story of my journey — a tale of the truest affection.'

Gorem stepped towards the divan upon which Amberine was reclining.

'From that wretched forest in the Kingdom of Unfortunate Salvation, I have brought the object of your dreams

— the one thing that touches all the senses.'

Her interest piqued, Amberine forced a smile.

As she did so, Gorem held up an ordinary acorn.

'I am sorry to tell you, that is not the object of my dreams,' said Amberine.

The second of my ghoul brothers, Sorem, went next.

'I may be deaf, but my inability to hear is the reason I'll win the hand of my lovely bride-to-be,' he said. 'Unlike my brothers standing beside me, I am not hindered by the follies besetting those born with hearing. As such, I was able to hone my other senses on the adventure, and to perceive the true nature of the quest.

'I travelled west, along the snaking river, through a succession of dominions and kingdoms. Guided by the kindness of strangers and by a burning zeal to succeed, I followed a long, twisting trail of clues.

'For weeks and months I wandered, until at last I came to a mountain as towering as any other in the Kingdom of Glorious Redemption. An informant there had revealed that a jinn, residing on an uppermost slope, could answer any question posed by a troubled mind.

'And he was right. For, as I was to discover, the most terrible creature imaginable existed there. He would have surely devoured me. But, thinking fast, I begged forgiveness for trespassing, and recounted to him the story of my journey — a tale of the truest affection.'

Sorem stepped towards the divan upon which Amberine was reclining.

'From that wretched slope in the Kingdom of Glorious Redemption, I have brought the object of your dreams — the one thing that touches all the senses.'

Her interest piqued, Amberine forced a smile.

As she did so, Sorem held up an ordinary pebble.

'I am sorry to tell you, that is not the object of my dreams,' said Amberine.

My third ghoul brother, Korem, went next.

'I may not have the power of smell, but the lack of an olfactory nerve is the reason I'll win the hand of my lovely bride-to-be,' he said. 'Unlike my brothers standing beside me, I am not hindered by the follies besetting those born with a sense of smell. As such, I was able to hone my other senses on the adventure, and to perceive the true nature of the quest.

'I travelled south, along the snaking river, through a succession of dominions and kingdoms. Guided by the kindness of strangers and by a burning zeal to succeed, I followed a long, twisting trail of clues.

'For weeks and months I wandered, until at last I came to a desert as wide as any other in the Kingdom of Darkest Firmament. An informant there had revealed that a jinn, residing at a small oasis in the centre of the vast wilderness, could answer any question posed by a troubled mind.

'And he was right. For, as I was to discover, the most terrible creature imaginable existed there. He would have surely devoured me. But, thinking fast, I begged forgiveness for trespassing, and recounted to him the story of my journey — a tale of the truest affection.'

Korem stepped towards the divan upon which Amberine was reclining.

'From that fearful desert in the Kingdom of Darkest Firmament, I have brought the object of your dreams — the one thing that touches all the senses.'

Her interest piqued, Amberine forced a smile.

As she did so, Korem held up a handful of sand.

'I am sorry to tell you, that is not the object of my dreams,' said Amberine.

The fourth of my ghoul brothers, Porem, went next.

'I may not have a sense of touch, but my inability to feel is the reason I believe I shall win the hand of my lovely bride-to-be,' he said. 'Unlike my brothers standing beside me, I am not hindered by the follies besetting those born with feeling. As such, I was able to hone my other senses on the adventure, and to perceive the true nature of the quest.

'I travelled north, along the snaking river, through a succession of dominions and kingdoms. Guided by the kindness of strangers and by a burning zeal to succeed, I followed a long, twisting trail of clues.

'For weeks and months I wandered, until at last I came to an inland sea in the Kingdom of Slaked Thirst. An informant

there had revealed that a jinn, residing on an island in the middle of the sea, could answer any question posed by a troubled mind.

'And he was right. For, as I was to discover, the most terrible creature imaginable existed there. He would have surely devoured me. But, thinking fast, I begged forgiveness for trespassing, and recounted to him the story of my journey — a tale of the truest affection.'

Sorem stepped towards the divan upon which Amberine was reclining.

'From that wretched island in the Kingdom of Slaked Thirst, I have brought the object of your dreams — the one thing that touches all the senses.'

Her interest piqued, Amberine forced a smile.

As she did so, Porem held up a coconut.

'I am sorry to tell you, that is not the object of my dreams,' said Amberine.

The fifth of my ghoul brothers, Dorem, went last.

'I may be unable to taste, but my inability to do so is the reason I believe I shall win the hand of my lovely bride-to-be,' he said. 'Unlike my brothers standing beside me, I am not hindered by the follies besetting those born with taste. As such, I was able to hone my other senses on the adventure, and to perceive the true nature of the quest.

'I travelled south-east, along the snaking river, through a succession of dominions and kingdoms. Guided by the kindness of strangers and by a burning zeal to succeed, I followed a long, twisting trail of clues.

'For weeks and months I wandered, until at last I came to an ocean as endless as any other between the Kingdom of Insufferable Damnation and eternity. An informant there had revealed that a jinn, residing in the ocean, could answer any question posed by a troubled mind.

'And he was right. For, as I was to discover, the most terrible creature imaginable existed there. He would have surely devoured me. But, thinking fast, I begged forgiveness for trespassing, and recounted to him the story of my journey — a tale of the truest affection.'

Dorem stepped towards the divan upon which Amberine was reclining.

'From that wretched ocean in the Kingdom of Insufferable Damnation, I have brought the object of your dreams

— the one thing that touches all the senses.'

Her interest piqued, Amberine forced a smile.

As she did so, Dorem held up a phial filled with sea water.

'I am sorry to tell you, that is not the object of my dreams,' said Amberine.

Once all five of my ghoul siblings had spoken, my father and mother rose to their feet. They both seemed a little embarrassed that their five sons had been unable to win the heart of the woman they all so adored.

Just before the assembly was adjourned, I stood up and knelt before Amberine.

'I am the youngest of the brothers,' I said, 'and I confess that I have neither embarked on a journey, nor returned from one. But, despite the lack of miles to have passed beneath my feet, I believe I know the object of your dreams.'

Her interest piqued, Amberine forced a smile, as she had already done five times.

'I think we have taken enough of the young lady's time,' my father said curtly.

'She's surely tired of this game,' my mother added.

But, sitting up, Amberine held out a delicate hand of invitation.

'All five of your siblings have regaled us with their tales,' she said, 'and so it is only fair that you should have a turn to speak.'

Still kneeling, and giving thanks, I expressed my mind.

'I believe I know that the object of your dreams — the one thing that touches all the senses — is true love.'

Hearing the words, Amberine gasped, her eyes welling with tears.

'You may not be ripened by adventure,' she said, 'but you are the only man in the world I would ever wish to marry.'

And so, that's how I was matched with the most wonderful woman in all the world.

HOURGLASS

Eight strangers were clustered
around the campfire
of the caravanserai —
silhouetted, ragged, and
ripened by adventure.
As the flames licked
the darkness, sparks
spitting up into the desert's
nocturnal firmament,
the traveller dressed in
indigo cleared his throat
and told his tale:

ONE MORNING IN late summer, when I
was a child of ten, my father led me into
the meadow.

As the sun warmed us gently, we sat
down on the long grass and breathed in
the scent of nature. I remember the scene
as though it were etched into my mind,
having relived it a thousand times in the
years since.

There are two reasons I cherish that
memory as I do.

The first is that it was a blissful moment
alone with the wisest, kindest man in all
the world.

The second reason is as sorrowful as
the first is blissful.

You see, as we lay back in the grass,
my father told me something that was to
shape both his life and mine.

'Listen well, my little gazelle,' he said, as I played with the bow and arrow he'd made for me.

'What is it, Baba?'

'I have something to explain.'

My father looked at me in a way he hadn't looked at me before. As he did so, his eyes welled with tears.

'When my father turned thirty, he died,' he said. 'And his father died at precisely the same age, as did his father, and his father before him.'

I would have smiled, imagining the sentence was the beginning of a joke, but I soon realized it was not.

Pulling me onto his belly, my face close to his, he said:

'Next week is my thirtieth birthday.'

'That's so old, Baba,' I said.

My father shook his head.

'It may seem so to a young fellow like you, but it's not.'

As I peered into his eyes, tears rolled down his cheeks.

'Are you going to die next week, Baba?' I asked.

'Perhaps.'

A veil of gloom descended over my face, and I felt sick.

'But why, Baba?'

'Because all the men of our line die when they reach this age.'

I caressed my hand through his hair.

'Are you sick, Baba?'

'No. Not at all. I feel as strong as an ox.'

'Then you'll live till you are older than old, Baba,' I whispered. 'I know you will!'

As we lay there, basking in sunlight, my father made me promise him something.

'Promise me that you will do as I have done,' he said. 'Study hard, get married young, and have a little boy just like you.'

'I promise, Baba,' I said.

Arm in arm, we left the meadow and walked back through the orchards.

When we reached our little home, I reached out and squeezed my father's hand, looked him in the eye, and said:

'Don't die, Baba.'

But he did.

Three days after that morning in the meadow, he fell down and never got up.

My mother cried for days and nights, as we all did.

After the funeral, my brother heard a neighbour in the village say we were cursed. I yelled out that I'd go and punch them.

'You are only ten years old,' my mother said. 'So you're not going to punch anyone.'

'Well, I'll punch them when I'm older,' I barked.

'No,' my mother said. 'When you're older, you're not going to do any punching either.'

'Why not?'

'Because you are going to spend your life working out why all the men of your line die at exactly the same age — an age far too young to ascend to the heavens.'

Ten summers came and went.

A decade in which I learned logic and mathematics, languages, science, and even the art of navigation.

One evening, just as I was opening a book on celestial navigation, my mother came to me.

In her hand was a tattered canvas bag with leather straps.

'This is for you,' she said. 'It was your father's when he was your age, and your grandfather's before him.'

She paused, stroked a hand to my cheek, and added a line that never leaves my thoughts:

'They used it on their journey to learn the secret of why their lives were destined to be so short.'

I swallowed hard.

'Where did they look?'

My mother sighed.

'Everywhere.'

'And did they arrive at any answers?'

'None. So they accepted their lot, returned home, and...'

Breaking down into a flood of tears, my mother pushed the canvas bag towards me.

The next morning I left the village and went in search of the reason why the men of my direct line never lived beyond the age of thirty.

Most people who embark on a quest usually have a clear route in mind, or at least an agenda. Most people would have looked at the maps before leaving home and talked to others who had been to the destination.

But my journey was different.

I had no idea where I was going, or what I would do when I got there.

All I knew was that, with each sunset and sunrise, the years, months, and weeks of my life were disappearing.

I travelled from one kingdom to the next, spoke to wise men, sorcerers, soothsayers, and even witches. I took advice from highwaymen and madmen, climbed up mountains, and crossed oceans.

But never once did I get the feeling I was close to an answer.

Seven years, seven months, and seven days since leaving my village, I reached a fondouk perched on a hillside on the Mongolian Steppe. It was bitterly cold, and late by the time I had tended to my mules.

Taking refuge inside the fondouk, I shared a little of my tale with another traveller.

Like me, he hailed from far away.

'You are hurrying through life,' he said, 'because you are so anxious about what may come. But in your quest for answers, you have crossed half the known world, and lived a dozen lives.'

For the first time in my grand adventure, I reflected.

The traveller was right.

I had made a great journey, and it had made me.

Before turning in for the night, I asked my fellow adventurer if he had any suggestions for a wandering soul such as myself.

'Go up to the mountain,' he said, 'and search for the hermit who lives in a cleft that's little bigger than himself.'

The traveller tapped me on the knee.

'I'll tell you a secret,' he said. 'There's no hermit wiser in all the world than Dambyn the Wise.'

Certain that I was setting off on yet another misadventure, I made ready the mules long before the dawn light had brought a blush of colour to the vast and empty landscape.

I travelled for a day, and then another, the great mountain looming larger as I trudged ahead.

On the third day, I left the mules, packed a few provisions in the canvas bag my mother had given me, and began the weary ascent.

I might have stopped and given up, but something goaded me on — the stirring voice of my father ringing in my ears.

'Do it for your son, and his son, and his son!'

Exhausted and frozen to the bone, I spied a ledge up near the summit.

Pushing myself harder than I've ever been pushed, I covered the last stretch and reached the cleft in which the hermit lived.

Dambyn the Wise was so old that his skin was hanging off his bones. He didn't seem in the least surprised to find me there.

I began to explain why I had come.

He held out an ancient hand, the long, tapered fingers pointing like an arrowhead at my chest.

'I know why you are here,' he said gruffly.

I shook my head.

'No, no, I am sure you do not,' I answered. 'You see, every man in my direct line—'

'Drops dead soon after he has travelled thirty times around the sun.'

47

My frozen brow furrowed.

'Will you help me?' I asked, the words hardly audible.

'Provide the payment.'

'I have almost nothing to my name, sir. Three weary mules down in the valley, and a few provisions.'

The hermit rolled his eyes.

'That isn't the kind of payment I require.'

'Then, what is it?'

'Tell me a promise, a secret, and a wish.'

'A promise…?'

'You heard what I said.'

My mind numb, I strained to think.

'A promise: To study hard, get married young, and have a little boy as I was. A secret: In all the world, there's no hermit wiser than Dambyn the Wise.'

'And a wish?'

I rubbed a hand down over my face.

'I wish for an end to the torment that besets my line.'

The hermit held out an index finger and beckoned me into the tiny cleft in which he had resided since his youth.

Before I could ask whether he knew the answer to my dilemma, he told me that he did.

'You must travel to such-and-such a place,' he uttered in a slow, cold tone. 'And, when you get there, you must clear your mind and forget why you have come. Follow the instructions I will give you, and do not deviate from them, or else you shall fail.'

'But what if I follow them to the letter?'

The hermit sniffed the air.

'Then you will gain an answer to the question that consumes you.'

'But what of a solution — will I gain a solution as well?'

'That, young man, is up to you.'

So, promising to obey the instructions as I had been given them, I left the hermit's cleft.

Having retraced the route back down the mountainside, I trekked with my mules over a dozen horizons, and then a dozen more. After many weeks and months, I reached the destination which Dambyn the Wise had described in words.

As you can imagine, I have sworn an oath not to divulge the location — suffice to say, it was not where I expected it to be.

Indeed, it could not have been in a less likely place.

Following the orders to the letter, I reached a battered oak door, the outer surface gnawed by time and the elements.

Mindful not to deviate from the instructions I had been given, I performed the ritual expected of one hoping to gain entry.

Against the noise of iron wheels grinding, the portal disappeared into the ground.

I stepped inside.

As soon as I had done so, the portal was raised once again.

An ordinary passageway delivered me to the most extraordinary place that surely exists in all the heavens, the worlds, and the hells.

As for the dimensions — they were not bound by the limits of the human mind, but rather inspired by the infinite.

I had entered a chamber, or whatever it was, with no visible walls, ceiling, or floor.

I stepped forwards onto a kind of iron gantry. One of thousands, it was an insignificant part of a vast scaffolding.

Every available inch of space was filled with that orderly iron framework.

And, in turn, every inch of it was taken up by hourglasses — millions of them, hanging in lines on what looked like meat hooks.

Twice the length of man's hand, the objects were uniform in appearance. On closer inspection, I noticed that each one was inscribed with a name.

Some of the devices had only just been turned.

Others were nearing the end of an interval between a beginning and an end.

As I stood there, marvelling at what my eyes were showing me, I noticed the silhouette of a man zigzagging his way along the lines of hourglasses.

Peering at the sand, he would wait until the last grains drained from north to south.

As soon as the upper portion of the hourglass was empty, he would unhook it, mumble what I assumed was a prayer, and hurl it into the abyss.

Then he would watch as a fresh hourglass moved into place.

Fascinated right down to the marrow of my bones, I stepped towards the figure.

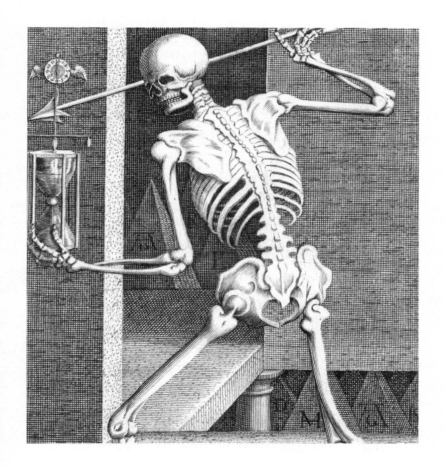

On hearing the sound of feet approaching, he spun round into the light. I swear he turned into a skeleton for a moment, as though to frighten me — as if his usual incarnation were not fearful enough.

Bloodshot and disbelieving, a single eye dominated the face.

A pair of jagged horns poked out from the matted hair above, and a third one from his chin. As that great eye focussed on me, I spat out the password that had opened the portal.

'What is your business here?' he enquired in a gruff tone.

I explained how every male member of my line was struck down as soon as they had lived the sunrises of thirty years.

'I have tramped across the known and unknown world,' I said. 'I have traversed mountain ranges, oceans, deserts, and seas and, at last, I am here.'

The creature motioned for me to be silent.

Peering into the sands of a man's life, he unhooked an hourglass, threw it into the abyss, and watched as another slid into position.

'How long have you searched for answers?' he asked.

In thought, I touched a fingertip to my chin.

'For ten years,' I answered. 'I was twenty when I left my village and…' As if being strangled, I gasped. 'In all my wandering I forgot.'

'*Forgot?*'

'Forgot that this very day marks thirty years upon this earth.'

The creature asked my name, that of my father, and his father before him.

As soon as the names had been both spoken and heard, he led me up and down, along and then back again.

We passed millions and millions of hourglasses — each one of which presumably represented a human life.

There were, it seemed, thousands of creatures engaged in that most peculiar work. I dared not ask, but assumed they were jinns.

All of a sudden, the creature stopped.

Leaning forward, he touched a claw to an hourglass with a great many years to run.

'This is you,' he said. 'And it's where your father, grandfather, and where your ancestors were born and died.'

'There's plenty of sand in it,' I said with relief.

As I spoke the words, I perceived the answer to the single question that dogged my ancestral line.

A vast and incomprehensible mechanism ruled over the chamber.

Half-mechanical and half-alive, it was powered by a series of colossal counterweights. Swinging to and fro through the abyss, they seemed somehow to keep the individual hourglasses in line with time itself.

The hook on which my life was suspended was out of alignment by a fraction of a fraction. Such was the enormity of that place, that the counterweight passed once in thirty years — smashing an hourglass and snuffing out a life each time it came around.

At the exact moment I solved the riddle, a pendulum wheeled out from nowhere, careening through the darkness.

The creature lunged forwards.

Making sense of what was about to occur, he shoved the hook backwards in the nick of time.

The counterweight arced up into the darkness, leaving the sands of my life to run and run.

I expressed the most sincere thanks.

The creature's single eye regarded me, then blinked.

As for me, for a good long while I stared at the grains of sand streaming through the neck of the hourglass.

I pondered all the lives that had come and gone in all the hourglasses, on all the hooks.

I gave thanks to providence for sparing me, and those who were to come.

Then, I turned on my heel and began the long journey home.

IMAGINIST

Eight strangers were clustered
around the campfire
of the caravanserai —
silhouetted, ragged, and
ripened by adventure.
As the flames licked
the darkness, sparks
spitting up into the desert's
nocturnal firmament,
the traveller dressed in
indigo cleared his throat
and told his tale:

MY FATHER USED to say I was born during a tempest, the storm clouds darker grey than any others he'd ever seen.

It may sound fanciful, but I have always imagined that, as I took my first pained gasps for air, those brooding clouds were somehow born inside me.

The reason is that, throughout my childhood and much of my life, I was known by everyone as 'Grey Man'.

I loved that shade, took solace in it, and took pleasure in having it as my name.

The other children would be dressed in vibrant hues, while I begged my mother to allow me wear grey. I would choose books to read which had grey covers and grey diagrams, and would search out grey food. I only went out at twilight, when the city, and the landscape beyond, were as grey as a sketch in charcoal.

The grey life suited me, for I was comforted by the one tone that appeared to be as fond of me as I was of it.

On completing my studies, I was apprenticed to a blacksmith. Working at the forge from morning till night, my face, arms, and hands were habitually as grey as my clothing.

Each night when I fell asleep, I would slip into dreams of monotone, devoid of any colour at all. My imagined adventures were played out against a grey backcloth, just as I yearned for them to be.

Then, one night, I went to bed as normal, having eaten a pomegranate given to me by a friend of a friend. The fruit was delicious, and unusually large. Getting under the covers, I thanked providence for my life and my

friendships, and fell into a deep, child-like sleep.

That night, my dreams exploded into a cornucopia of dazzling colours.

As Grey Man, I hardly knew how to describe such concoctions of raw beauty.

It was as though every cell in my body had been jolted alive.

My mind was washed in effervescent yellows and haunting pinks, reds as savage as the blood of battle, radiant topaz, moss green, blues as dark as lapis lazuli flecked with gold, and fabulous indigo, such as the robe that shrouds me on this very night.

The next morning, I woke up feeling that my head had been trampled by a cohort of savage jinns.

My throat was swollen, and my mouth was raw.

As the lids lifted from my bloated eyes, I let out a cry of consternation.

The room in which my bed was situated had been deluged in colour — reds, purples, greens, yellows, and all the hues of a conjurer's imagination. Certain that I'd gone insane, I went to see a celebrated alchemist in his busy workshop.

As he listened, I explained how I'd consumed an especially delicious pomegranate the evening before.

Through a lens the alchemist peered into the left eye, then the right. He looked at my tongue, felt my head, and shrugged.

'Are you feeling feverish?' he asked.

I shook my head from side to side.

'Any numbness in your hands?'

'No.'

The alchemist screwed up his eyes until they were lost in creases.

'How is your imagination?' he asked.

'My what?'

'Your imagination.'

'That's a curious question.'

'I know it is... but just answer it... Try to imagine a desert island with a forest beside the beach.'

I closed my eyes.

As if my mind had been cued to do so, I spied a tropical paradise with sand as white as chalk. Rising up behind the beach was a jungle, seething with life.

Holding a hand to shade my eyes, I scanned the distance from one horizon to the next.

I was completely alone.

Elated, and yet fearful, something deep inside me caused me to fret.

Before I had any chance to stop it, my mind's eye imagined a giant prehistoric predator tearing across the beach.

And there it was...

A beast sculpted by my imagination, conjured into being as if in a dream.

The size of a bull elephant, its body was scaled like an armadillo, armoured with talons, tusks, and fangs.

My leg muscles clenching tight, I ran as fast as I have ever run... hurtling forwards over the powdered white sand in a bid to reach the jungle.

But, despite my speed, the predator breached the distance between us.

Even though it was behind me, I could see it, hear it, smell it, and even feel it.

The great mouth opened, and I spied row upon row of monstrous teeth.

Just before the creature from the farthest reaches of hell bore down on me, I heard a voice.

'Do you see it — the desert island?'

Jerked back to the present, I looked deep into the alchemist's eyes.

'That fantasy was more real than anything I have ever experienced,' I said.

The scientist nodded.

'I have witnessed this malaise once before,' he intoned. 'A child not yet five summers old, but with an imagination to rival any there's ever been.'

'Did he eat a poisoned pomegranate, like me?'

'Your condition is not due to a piece of fruit,' he said. 'Rather, it's the result of being cursed by someone jealous of the life you live.'

'I wonder who that could be,' I said, giving voice to my inner thoughts.

'What matters is not the malady but the cure,' the alchemist said.

Again, I regarded him in desperation.

'And what is the cure?' I enquired, my mind awash with colours — millions and millions of colours.

'In the case of the child of whom I have spoken, the remedy was to drain the potency of the disorder.'

'And how, may I ask, is that done?'

The alchemist stepped over to the window and glanced down at the street.

'By passing the imagination on,' he said.

I reminded him that, as a humble blacksmith who had clung to a colourless world all my life, I had no expertise in the workings of the human mind.

'Listen with care to what I am about to tell you,' the scientist said, 'and you will have a hope of being cured.'

So, I listened.

When the appointment was over, I paid the fee and promised to follow the steps of the remedy to the letter.

Accordingly, I made my way to the sign-writer and commissioned him to craft a simple sign, painted in many colours.

It read, simply:

IMAGINATION FOR SALE

Then, as I had been instructed to do, I took the sign and went to sit on a rug in the market square.

That evening, as the call to the faithful rang out over the city, I offered my services in exchange for a single dinar.

It wasn't long before the first customer hurried up.

A tall, squalid-looking man with a limp, he clicked his tongue at the sign, then at me.

'What's this all about?' he asked gruffly.

'Like it says, I am in the business of imagination.'

'But imagination isn't like meat or cheese! You can't buy and sell it just like that!'

'Yes, you can,' I answered. 'And if you don't believe me — pay your money and go home with a little imagination.'

Someone else, who had overheard the conversation, tossed a dinar coin onto my lap.

'I'm ready,' he said.

Thanking him for his faith in me, I reached out and pressed my hand to his brow.

Nothing happened at first, which caused the first man to renew his scorn.

But then, all of a sudden, the customer fell backwards, his eyes lighting up like a bright star on the dark night.

'I imagined an underwater kingdom filled with mermaids!' he exclaimed. 'There were chests of buried treasure, palaces carved from rock-crystal, and seahorses bedecked in the livery of a Scorpion Queen!'

Someone else stepped forward, paid their money, and asked for a dose of imagination.

Then another.

And fifty more.

By the end of the night, I had sold imagination to dozens of happy customers.

Word spread that an imaginist was offering escape from the dismal realities of life — universal problems for which our despotic ruler was directly responsible.

Next morning, when I pitched my hand-painted sign in the same place as the day before, a queue of people quickly formed.

The first person to whom I sold imagination was an elderly woman.

She asked me to enable her to imagine her childhood once again — a place of idyllic refuge she longed for in old age.

'It's for you to imagine what you wish to see,' I answered, placing my hand on her brow. 'Close your eyes and imagine you are exactly when, where, and who you wish to be.'

The tired old lids drooped over the tired old eyes, and the ancient giggled at the memory of her youth — a memory she relived as though it were being experienced for the very first time.

Through the long, hot day I provided my services, bringing light and delight to those who had not experienced joy in far too long a while.

As expected, quacks set themselves up, pretending to be imaginists, too.

But as soon as they were discovered to be charlatans, they were chased away.

On the seventh day since waking in a world ablaze in colour, the market place was cleared by the royal guard.

Armed with lances and swords, soldiers threatened to imprison anyone who disobeyed their orders to disperse.

The snaking line of people vanished, leaving me alone on my rug.

Before I knew it, soldiers had snatched me, marched me to a wagon, and thrown me in a dungeon beneath the palace.

In all the years I had lived, I had never imagined a place so sapped of colour. There was a time when I would have hailed it as the ultimate sanctuary. But, in my incarnation as an imaginist, it felt as though I had been robbed of sight.

And so, as I sat in that abhorrent cell, I closed my eyes and I imagined like I had never imagined before.

I was transported to a kingdom poised at the edge of the world, in which all the men were trees, and the trees were men.

The rain fell upwards from the ground to the sky; the butterflies were the size of soup bowls, and the moon sang lullabies more lovely than any I have heard.

As time passed, I found that I could control the imaginary world in which I had arrived so keenly that it was as if I was actually there. Rather than appear as the foreigner that I was, I simply honed my imagination so as to blend in.

On one occasion when a tree-turned-man commented on my accent, I simply responded that I'd begun life as an acorn beyond the Topaz Desert.

I have no idea how long I dallied in that bewitching realm.

What I do know is that the intoxicating experience came to an abrupt end when the jailer unlocked the iron door.

A pair of soldiers from the royal guard seized me from the corner in which I was huddled.

One of them threw a bucket of water over me. The other drew a sword from its scabbard.

'Misbehave and I'll slit your throat,' he warned.

Marched at double speed up from the dungeons, I was kicked down at the feet of the king.

Bald as an egg, with a long chin and a waxy complexion, the monarch possessed cruel, dark eyes.

'Are you the imaginist of which my spies have been jabbering?'

I shrugged, then nodded.

'I suppose I am.'

'Tell me, then,' the ruler growled, 'what is the most extraordinary thing you can imagine?'

I closed my eyes and watched as a glorious mirage swept onto the stage of my mind.

'I can imagine a kingdom in which all the people are happy,' I said. 'A place bathed in a vivid array of colours, it's a land of abundant happiness and joy, governed by a king who's loved by every man, woman, and child.'

The king grinned.

'You describe my own fair kingdom,' he said.

'Your Majesty,' I responded gently, 'an imaginist has no interest in imagining that which exists.'

The despot appeared gravely displeased by the comment. I swear he was about to order for my head to be detached from my shoulders, when a vizier whispered in his ear.

'My detractors say I am merciless,' the monarch intoned. 'But, on the contrary, I am reasonable. To prove it, I shall allow you to perform your imagination.'

Getting to my feet, I reached a hand towards the king's brow.

Fearing I was about to strike, a guard knocked me to the ground.

'No one touches His Majesty!' the vizier declared.

With no other choice, I cupped my hands together as though holding an imaginary orange.

Then, with care, I blew into them, as the king and his courtiers looked on. Closing my eyes for a moment, I imagined myself throwing a ball of energy in the direction of the king.

Right away, the despot's eyes gleamed like burning coals — not with malice or greed, but with the strains of imagination.

In providing my service to others, I had not been curious as to their personal reveries. But, being in the palace, I admit curiosity took hold.

Closing my eyes, I allowed myself to peer into the depths of the king's troubled mind, and his equally troubled imagination.

And what a scene it was.

Our despotic leader was standing on the brow of a hill, staring out at the kingdom to the north — a dominion ruled by a kindly king.

Sucking up as much of my imagination as he could manage, he had imagined a vast army.

These were not merely legions of men, however — rather they were mechanical elephants, each one a fortress in its own right.

As I looked on, the spectral militia decimated the opposing force.

When it was over, the tyrant lifted the lids from his eyes, wiped away the tears of joy, and ordered for me to be returned to the cell from which I had come.

Over the weeks that followed, I slipped through the keyhole of my own imagination and journeyed through a thousand lands that existed nowhere else but in my mind.

One night, my imagining was interrupted by the sound of a voice coming from the next cell.

'Brother! Brother! Have you heard?'

'Have I heard what?'

'That wretched king of ours made a clockwork army — which has just been destroyed by the army from the north.'

An hour passed, and then every cell in the dungeon was opened.

Along with all the other prisoners, I was freed by the kindly soldiers from the next kingdom.

Then, as though it were too perfect an ending, that loathsome king of ours, now in chains, was thrown into the cell in which I myself had festered.

As for my imagination, it eventually did drain away, just as the alchemist had said it would.

My friends no longer called me 'Grey Man', but rather 'The Imaginist'.

JINN'S TREASURE

*Eight strangers were clustered
around the campfire
of the caravanserai —
silhouetted, ragged, and
ripened by adventure.
As the flames licked
the darkness, sparks
spitting up into the desert's
nocturnal firmament,
the traveller dressed in
indigo cleared his throat
and told his tale:*

I CONSIDER MYSELF to be attentive in my work, my friendships, and in the way I proceed through the twists and turns of life.

And so it was all the more alarming to step on a nail as I disembarked the dhow at Alexandria.

Sticking out proud from the deck, that grim splinter of iron was as thick as a human finger.

In great pain, I was taken to a surgeon in the backstreets of the city.

A hadji with a chalk-white beard down to his navel, he took one look at the wound and grunted.

'I'll amputate,' he said.

Recoiling, I protested:

'No one's going to chop off my foot, least of all you!'

'Well if you wish to keep it, you'll have to bathe it in vinegar infused with mercury.'

'What if I don't?'

The would-be surgeon glared at me hard with his good eye.

'Leave it untreated,' he said, 'and you will be dead within a week.'

Placing myself in the hands of God, I left the quack to his potions and his saw, and went to stay with my brother on the far side of the city.

Days of merriment came and went, in which stories of our youth were told and retold.

Rose water was sprinkled over hands, great platters of food served, and yet more tales were dusted off from memories and given voice.

And in all that time, I neglected the wound in my foot.

Exactly a week after my arrival at Alexandria, I woke to find the bedding on which I had been sleeping strewn with what looked like ink.

Dark blue ink — the hue of fermented indigo.

Amused more than I was alarmed, I did my best to trace the source of the dye.

Having hunted high and low, I gave up and went to the street fountain to wash.

Crouching there, making my ablutions, I spied the very same strain of blue washing out into the gutter.

Unable to understand what was taking place, I checked my clothing, my hands, and then my feet.

In astonishment, I saw that the indigo-coloured ink was streaming from the wound in my foot, as though my blood were dark blue.

However hard I washed it, more ink flowed out.

My back pressed against the fountain, I examined the injury.

Holding my foot into the light, I observed how large droplets of what looked like ink exited the injury one by one.

I cursed the nail, then the quack who'd been so keen to amputate.

After that, I dried the lesion and bound it tightly in a blinding white strand of cotton.

By midday, the bandage was soaked through with the dark blue ink, causing me grave alarm.

Fearing my troubles were not so much medical as spiritual, I sought out an astrologer near the great mosque.

Observing the indigo-soaked bandage, she reached for the Holy Book and kissed it seven times.

'I simply trod on a nail,' I said.

The hag shook her head from side to side.

'You *think* you trod on a nail,' she responded. 'In actual fact you stepped on a jinn.'

'What am I to do?'

Breathing in deeply through her mouth, the seer exhaled through her nostrils.

'You will have to wait,' she said.

'Wait for what?'

'For the jinn that has entered your life to make plain what he — or she — has in mind for you.'

'Can't I recite a certain prayer a hundred times, or sleep with an amulet tied around my neck?'

The soothsayer grimaced, her rotting teeth exposed to the light.

'You will wait,' she said.

And so, wait I did — for an entire week.

Each day, the ink spewing from my foot was a little darker and a little thicker than the day before.

Sitting on my bed, I would touch a hand to it.

Marvelling at the way its consistency was changing, I gave thanks that I wasn't in pain.

Another week slipped by.

Then, just as I was getting used to the bizarre condition, something took place that caused me fresh alarm.

I woke one morning to find a vertical line running from the injury, up my ankle, leg, and nether regions, to my torso.

Executed with perfection, it seemed to have been drawn by the hand of an artist.

Greatly intrigued, I pressed my chin down to my chest.

As I did so, an invisible quill, held in an equally invisible hand, began work on a pattern conjured in darkest indigo.

Swathing my entire abdomen, it seemed to be etching beneath the skin, as though the invisible artist were inside me.

Aghast, I watched in trepidation and awe.

What at first had appeared to be nothing more than a whimsical pattern was revealed to be a map.

Fearing the jinn inside me would be displeased were I not to fulfil its wishes, I ran through to the room in which my brother, Jamal, was about to take an afternoon nap.

In an urgent tone, I explained the sequence of events that had taken place since stepping on the nail.

Then, both bewildered and ashamed, I raised my robe.

'Dearest brother,' I said, fear shadowing my words, 'please tell me what manner of a thing is imprinted on my flesh.'

Never easily perturbed, my brother took a step back. Observing my belly,

he took in the intricate pattern covering every inch of skin.

'This is no ordinary map,' he said after a prolonged silence.

I glowered. 'Happy to hear it.'

His concentration sharp as a blade, Jamal looked me straight in the eye.

'From what I can see, it's a map leading to an immense treasure.'

'Why would a jinn wish to provide me with a treasure?' I cried. 'Surely it's a trick — the kind that aimless jinns are well known for playing.'

My brother held up a hand to pause my musings.

'It is clear the jinn has no intention of giving you the treasure,' he said.

'But, surely, if a jinn wished such a treasure,' I riposted, 'it would simply reach out and take it.'

His eyes masked in fear, my brother blinked.

'Not this treasure.'

'Why not?'

'Because this is the treasure of a demon.'

'So?'

'Well, as you may remember from the tales told to us as children, a code of honour exists between demons and jinns.'

'Where is the treasure?'

Jamal peered at my belly for a long while, taking in the many details.

He sighed.

'In a city beneath the sea.'

'It's insanity,' I said, the words as pained as my fear. 'Let's forget about the map, the treasure, the jinn, and the damned hole in my foot.'

Jamal shook his head — left, right, left.

'If ever there was a time to forget something and move briskly on with your life,' he responded, 'this is *not* it.'

'Then how do you suggest I reach the treasure, retrieve what is needed, and live to tell the tale?'

My dear brother peered at the map tattooed across my torso.

'All the details are there,' he said.

I thought for a moment.

'Very well. Tomorrow, I shall buy a full sheet of vellum in the market,' I said, 'and ask you to copy the map upon it. Then, placing myself in the hands of our ancestors, I shall set off to find the treasure.'

Accordingly, I ventured into the bazaar the next morning and purchased the finest sheet of vellum I could afford, along with reed nibs and ink.

That evening, Jamal bid me to lie down on the bed, as he prepared to copy the map.

Pen in hand, he scrutinized my belly, and gasped.

'I don't believe it,' he uttered in dismay.

'What is it?'

'The map has altered.'

'*Altered?*'

'Last night, it was quite different.'

'How so?'

'It was smaller, and...'

'*And,* what?'

Jamal's expression was one of utter disbelief.

'It's shifting,' he said. 'Even now, the details are shifting, as I watch them!'

'What do you mean?'

'Just as you yourself are living, so this infernal map is alive!'

I frowned.

'But then there is no point in copying the jinn's map.'

My brother cleared his throat.

'We shall travel together,' he said. 'As you would be there for me, so I shall be there for you.'

At dawn the next day, the two of us stole out from the house and began an adventure that was to alter the way we perceived the world.

We quickly learned that what we imagined to be reality was a fiction. And we came to appreciate that what we inhabited was nothing more than a meaningless backwater of nonsense.

Through days, nights, weeks, and many months, we followed the ever-changing contours of the map tattooed into my skin.

Each time it was consulted, the chart was new, as though an invisible force had redrawn it from the inside out.

We crossed deserts drier than any other, hacked our way through forests impenetrable and dark, battled with ogres, sang with sirens, and were even buried alive and thought the end had come.

Each time we stared our demise squarely in the face, an invisible hand seemed to pluck us from certain death when we least expected it.

Each time, we would marvel at our good fortune at yet another impossible escape.

And each time, Jamal would deliver a familiar line:

'We have survived because the jinn wished for us to do so, and for no other reason at all.'

By the time we reached the cavern's door, we were both matured, withered, aged, as though we had experienced ten thousand lives in one.

In any usual circumstances I might have detailed for you the catalogue of trials and tribulations, but this journey was different from others I have undertaken. It is as though speaking of the individual encounters would be to belittle them — as if they were meant for my memory, and mine alone.

All I shall say is that the cavern was located in the deepest part of the ocean — reached by a natural shaft that plunged straight down from the surface.

Indeed, the descent was so acute that both Jamal and I were subjected to terrible force.

As we climbed down, our skulls were almost cracked in by the pressure.

After rappelling downwards for what seemed like an eternity, we reached the cavern door...

What horror the mere thought of that portal projects across the stage of my mind.

Encrusted with barnacles and imprinted with death, it was as ready a warning as it was an entrance — threatening us to turn back for fear of being reduced to dust, as countless others had surely been.

Jamal looked at me hard, his bloodshot eyes more eloquent than the words of any language.

'If we manage to get through there,' I said, my voice hoarse, 'the only certainty is that we will not emerge the same as we are now.'

My dear brother leant forward and wiped a hand over my torso, inspecting the map, which was still changing.

He flinched.

'What is it?'

'It was blue and now it is red.'

Digging my chin into my chest, I looked for myself.

'Blood,' I said. '*My* blood — which explains why I feel faint.'

In a growl worthy of a bear woken from its hibernation, I called upon the jinn whom I'd troubled while quitting that wretched dhow so long before.

'We are here!' I snarled. 'Now it is for you to do what you need to do to gain the treasure, so that we may return to the lives we once enjoyed.'

Before I could utter another word, the portal vanished — obliterated by the necromancy of one given life by smokeless fire.

One moment, my brother and I were standing in the shaft, on the outer side of that damned portal.

The next, we were in a fantasy worthy of *Alf Layla wa Layla.*

A heartbeat after entering the chamber, both of us had forgotten every detail of the journey that had brought us there.

The details of anguish were as trivial to us as the thought of labour is to the lost souls of an opium den.

The treasure vault was large enough to accommodate an army ready for war. And yet, it seemed quite small —

because it was packed, floor to rafters, with sacks of gold, precious stones, and with artefacts of the most extraordinary nature.

Viewing that scene, I was grateful to have trodden on the nail as I had.

It may sound ludicrous, but I half-wished that in my time I had stepped on a hundred more such nails. Even if it had meant undergoing a hundred times the anguish, it would have been meagre payment for that vista of such astounding awe.

Turning an index finger towards myself, I touched it to the map.

'What is it the jinn wishes for?' I asked.

Jamal took in the details, as he had done over many months.

Tracing a fingertip along a line from my neck to the tip of my heel, he nodded.

'I understand,' he said in a flat voice.

'Understand *what*?'

'The jinn has explained what he wishes us to take.'

I shrugged.

'Tell me.'

My brother strode through the chamber, weaving a path between the objects and the piles of sacks.

A moment later, he was standing before me again.

Reaching a fist out in my direction, he opened his hand, a small conch shell on its palm.

'This,' he said.

'*That*? That's *all* he wants?'

Jamal blinked.

'We risked our lives a thousand times over, endured the unendurable, and *that* is all we're required to take?'

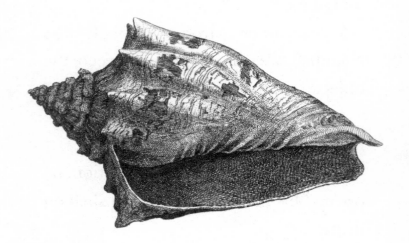

Again, my brother blinked.

'What foolish creatures are jinns,' I said, 'to waste their lives with such meaningless possessions.'

Jamal smiled. As he did so, he cast an eye over the cavern's immense treasure.

'What foolish creatures are humans,' he replied, 'to waste their lives with such meaningless possessions.'

Closing my fingers on the little conch shell, I jabbed a thumb at my torso, for my brother to check the proposed route of escape.

As the tip of my thumb touched my chest — the skin of which was tattooed with my blood as its ink — my ears filled with a deafening *whoosh*!

A fraction of a moment passed.

A thunderclap, followed by a lightning bolt.

Then, my lungs filling with air like those of a drowning man reaching the ocean's surface, I found myself standing in the parlour of my own home.

As bewildered as I, Jamal was standing beside me.

The map, which had festooned my body, had been erased.

I opened my clenched fist, but the conch shell — a sublime treasure of a jinn — was gone.

JINNLORE

Eight strangers were clustered
around the campfire
of the caravanserai —
silhouetted, ragged, and
ripened by adventure.
As the flames licked
the darkness, sparks
spitting up into the desert's
nocturnal firmament,
the traveller dressed in
indigo cleared his throat
and told his tale:

THE SPARKS OF the fire coaxing my memory, and the stars above as my witness, I am reminded of a summer two-thirds of a lifetime ago.

In my youth, I was foolish and brash, the kind of young man who challenged others to brawl with me in the streets because I had not the intelligence to know better. Little more than a simpleton, and raw through and through, I was scarred from head to toe and scared of nothing.

My mother used to scold me for not getting an honest job and whenever my father returned from his travels, he would rue the day I was born.

In return, I'd rail against my family and their coterie for being wretched, weak, the kind of people who lived hollow lives.

One morning, before the moon was asleep and the sun awake, I crept from the house in which we lived and made my way out to the open road.

My blood was fortified with the energy of youth and by stupidity, for I believed nothing was beyond me.

As I took my first steps on that pitted track, I spied the silhouettes of the farmers in the fields, and I scorned them one by one.

What pitiful examples of empty life to be content with the hand fate had dealt them.

All morning I tramped towards the horizon and all afternoon I thanked providence for giving me an opportunity to prove myself.

Strolling ahead, I thought of the village where I had been born, and of all the imbeciles I had known — imbeciles I'd left in my wake.

With dusk approaching, I wondered where to find a meal and to shelter for the night. In my enthusiasm for escape I hadn't given a second thought to taking along a blanket or provisions.

The moon ascended behind a screen of poplars, its macabre light stretching my shadow.

Hungry and weary, I cursed myself for not giving better forethought to my adventure — a life lesson in itself.

As I did so, I heard a voice:

'There's food and shelter in the shack beyond the trees.'

'Who's there?!' I called out in alarm.

'A friend.'

Spinning around, I hunted urgently for the form whose lips had seemed so close.

'You're evidently near enough to touch, so why can't I see you?'

'Because I am invisible.'

'Are you a spirit?'

'As I told you, I am a friend,' the voice explained. 'That is all you need to know.'

Even hungrier and more tired than before, and with no other solutions to remedy my predicament, I ventured in the direction of the poplar trees and found the shack of which the voice had spoken.

Laid out on a low table inside was a meal fit for a king. There were roasted kebabs on beds of fragrant rice, tureens of stewed aubergines and pumpkin,

platters of exotic fruits, and jugs of the most delicious sherbet I had ever tasted.

Without pausing to offer thanks, I devoured as much as I could.

Then, my belly distended with greed, I lay down to sleep on the mattress arranged beside a roaring log fire.

All night I tossed and turned, my sleep disrupted by crazed thoughts inspired by mania. I imagined I was a grotesque ghoul being hunted by an army of townsfolk through a forest, burning torches in their hands.

Next morning, I awoke in the rain.

The mattress and the fire were gone, as was the low table and the remnants of the feast, and the shack.

My clothing was ripped to shreds, my feet bare, and my skin was bloodied, as though it had been slashed with knives.

Groaning and reeling, I clambered to my feet and staggered ahead on the open road.

Within an hour or two I came upon a cottage, smoke streaming up from its chimney. Hurrying forwards, I thumped at the door.

I heard voices inside. Then the door opened, a farmer standing in its frame.

As soon as he set eyes upon me, he cried out in horror — as though he had set eyes on a spectre from another world.

Brandishing a blade, he swore upon all he held sacred to dispatch me if I were not gone within the blink of an eye.

Turning on my bare heel, I ran.

I ran and ran, and ran and ran... with no idea what had occurred, or why I should cause such distress to a fellow human.

Having slept in a ditch on the second night, I reached a town nestled in the foothills of the great mounts.

Hopeful of finding somewhere to rest, I made my way to the first inn I saw.

As soon as I entered, everyone inside froze stock-still.

Time slowed to a trickle. Some people screamed, while others leapt up to guard their kith and kin.

Taking flight, I fled once again, as a muffled call to arms rang out far behind.

Through the streets I bounded, weeping at my wretched state, my skin bleeding.

With each minute that passed, the clamour of voices grew in the distance.

Faithful to my dream, they were coming for me — a fiery torch raised aloft in every fist.

Zigzagging through the streets, uncertain what to do or where to go, I took shelter behind a barrel.

My heart pounding as it had never pounded before, I listened to the sound of boots marching over the cobbles.

As that damned din grew louder and louder, and as the approaching flames licked the night, I heard a voice.

It was the voice that had provided me the feast, the voice that had led to all my woes.

'Hurry down the stairs behind you, and take shelter in the basement.'

'Leave me, you scoundrel!' I hissed. 'You're responsible for me crouching here in this terrible state!'

'Dally there for another moment,' the voice answered, 'and you'll be torn limb from limb.'

Shaking and bleeding, I did as the voice ordered and took shelter in the cellar. To my surprise, I found a sumptuous apartment inside, with a feather bed, a bathroom, and another meal fit for royalty.

Once I had eaten, I washed myself. In doing so, I caught sight of myself in the mirror mounted on the wall.

Never in all my adventures have I been so shaken as I was at spying my own face in that disc of burnished bronze.

As in my dream, I was a ghoul — my once-delicate features reduced to those of a monster.

Little wonder I was being hunted by the local populace.

'What have you done to me?' I yelled.

'It is what you have done to yourself,' the voice whispered back.

Sobbing like a child, I begged to be returned to my former life.

'There's no hope of that,' the voice answered.

'Why not?'

'Because you were not worthy of it.'

'Turn me back to how I was!' I exclaimed. 'I promise to be a better man than I was before!'

'There is only one way to regain the life you had known before,' the voice explained.

'Tell me, and I shall do it — whatever it takes!'

'Step through to the fireplace, and upon the mantel you will find a book. Read and obey the instructions you will find inside.'

Doing as the voice had bidden me, I strode through to the fireplace and picked the volume from the mantelpiece. Its leather covers touching my hands, the book seemed to warm, as though cognizant that it was being held.

Holding it to the light, I opened the cover and read the title: *Jinnlore*.

My concentration honed, I read page after page...

The tale was of a young man, much like myself, who had been selfish rather than selfless. Having brought shame on his family and their name, he abandoned all he knew and embarked on a journey.

After twists and turns, he ended up imprisoned in a fortress sculpted from porphyry, on the dark side of an island in the Slaked Sea of Damnation.

Gripped by the story, I turned the page to learn what became of the protagonist.

Transfixed, I read the last words aloud:

And then it was, that across the oceans and the mountains, the deserts and the seas, a young man with the outward form of a ghoul found himself at the last page of a book. Uncertain of what to think, he watched as a stone staircase was revealed in the floor beside him — a tangible link to his own destiny.

As I closed the volume, a stone staircase did indeed reveal itself.

Knowing that my fate lay beyond it, I cast an eye around the lodgings that had been so comfortable, and hurried down the stairs.

The journey which followed taught me to tell right from wrong, and that self-sacrifice is as worthy as self-importance is wicked.

Along the way, I learned to help those in need before they themselves had appreciated their need.

I learned to taste, feel, smell, hear, and to see for the first time in my life — not through the conceited senses of youth, but as a man.

Most important of all, I learned not to take, but to give in a way that fulfilled me far more than the one who received.

As I seeped up knowledge, the features of a ghoul softened and melted, returning my outward form to that of myself.

One night in late summer, I reached the Kingdom of Virtue, which had been overrun by a race of creatures known to the populace as 'bigornes'. Attacked with unknown ferocity, the people of that land sustained terrible casualties.

As a result, they had taken refuge in caves, having abandoned their homes.

Finding a stranger in their midst, every tongue in every mouth was asking what kind of a madman I was — to venture to a realm so terrorized.

Before I knew it, I was taken to the monarch, who was residing in a great galleried cavern on the leeward side of a mountain.

Beckoning me to draw close, the old man seemed dejected and forlorn.

'The bigornes have destroyed everything we ever had,' he said. 'Our army has been devoured, and all hope for our kingdom is lost.'

'Surely, Your Majesty, there is always hope,' I answered.

The king sighed.

'The only hope is to free the Blue Knight from the porphyry fortress beyond the Slaked Sea of Damnation.'

My eyes burning like coals, for the first time in my life I knew my destiny — it was stretching out like a path, awaiting my boots to walk upon it.

'I will free him and bring him here,' I said.

'But how will you ever find the fortress, let alone scale its walls?' the monarch asked.

'I have all the information I require,' I said, 'for it was contained in the pages of a book — a book whose end was the beginning of the journey that caused me to be kneeling here before you.'

Pledging not to rest until the Blue Knight had been freed, I left the cavern and set out for the Slaked Sea of Damnation.

Through days and nights, weeks and months, I crisscrossed the known world.

Halfway down a well that connected the surface to the very centre of the Earth, I obtained the password from an ifrit.

In the Labyrinth of Grim Reason, I milked the venom from the fangs of a dragon with sixteen heads, and twice as many tongues.

And, on the Mountain of Most Turbulent Suffering, I captured a rogue jinn named Zoq-Zoq that threatened the balance of space and time.

Moonrise followed sunset.

Sunrise followed moonset.

As fate and fear merged as one, I sailed across the Slaked Sea of Damnation.

Armed as I needed to be, I scaled the wall of the fortress, sculpted from porphyry, on the dark side of the island.

Climbing up onto the battlement, I found myself surrounded by stone warriors, an obsidian-tipped lance in every hand.

'Prepare for death!' their voices cried as one.

'I have ventured here to save the Blue Knight,' I bellowed, 'and on my lips is the password entrusted to me by an ifrit!'

As I had been instructed to do, I spoke the word forwards, backwards, and inside out.

The stone warriors brandished their lances in rage.

But then, just as they stormed towards me, they melted like butter thrown into a fire.

Making my entry into the fortress, I poured the venom obtained in the Labyrinth of Grim Reason onto the floor of the seventh passage I came to.

As soon as the last drop of the poison had soaked into the flagstones, a belching, sulphurous mist billowed out.

Rather than suffocating me, it enabled me to perceive the route ahead.

In less time than it takes to tell, I was standing at the door of the dungeon, behind which the Blue Knight was said to be kept prisoner.

From my pocket, I took the lead phial that contained the rogue jinn — captured at the mountain of Most Turbulent Suffering — and broke the seal.

Against a booming noise as mighty as a tempest, Zoq-Zoq billowed out.

'What is your wish, O Master?' he thundered.

'Open this door, so that I may free the Blue Knight!'

No sooner had my petition been spoken, than the portal vanished as dust.

I hurried forwards.

There was, however, no proud knight waiting inside.

But his robe and armour were there, laid out as though awaiting him.

Instead, I found a page torn from an ancient book — the very same book that had led me to the porphyry fortress:

Having become the man he was destined to be, the youth donned the costume of the Blue Knight. Then, on the wings of Zoq-Zoq, he returned to the Kingdom of Virtue and saved the populace from the bigornes, before departing on yet another adventure.

MELLIFIED MAN

*Eight strangers were clustered
around the campfire
of the caravanserai —
silhouetted, ragged, and
ripened by adventure.
As the flames licked
the darkness, sparks
spitting up into the desert's
nocturnal firmament,
the traveller dressed in
indigo cleared his throat
and told his tale:*

LIKE LOVE, THE sweet taste of honey lingers on the lips of those who have tasted it.

Ever since I was a small child, that sweet, unearthly offering of the bees was all I could think about.

My father kept a dozen hives down in the meadow, and my mother would mix a little of their harvest into every dish she served.

On long, hot summer nights I would bathe in water scented with royal jelly, and on dark winter mornings, I would rub beeswax into my skin.

At school, the other boys mocked me for smelling sweet. They said if I ate any more honey I'd grow wings and fly away.

Little did they know that, rather than filling me with sorrow, their taunting gave me hope...

Each night before bed, my brothers and sisters prayed for fine toys to play with, or to do well in school.

While they did so, I prayed to be transformed through a magical alchemy from a little boy into a honeybee.

The years passed...

Years in which my longing grew all the stronger.

As soon as I woke each morning, I'd hurry down to the meadow and sit beside the hives. As the bees set out to gather pollen, I would listen to them. It may sound fanciful to your ears, but I swear I could hear them speaking in a language of their own.

With the passing of the years, as I grew from a scrawny child into a young man, I learned their language. Unlike our own, the vernacular of the bees is a hybrid of a shrill droning buzz and an elaborate form of dance.

One scorching summer day when I was down at the hives, watching the bees dancing in and out, I sensed the cold shadow of a man fall over me.

Turning around, I set eyes on a wizened figure with a single eye, a ragged beard, and a face that looked as though it had endured a thousand lives.

'They like you,' he said in a voice as gentle as I had ever heard a stranger speak.

'They know me,' I replied, 'because I spend all the time I can down here.'

The stranger told me he was a farmer from a kingdom that lay across the mountains. Like me, he said he'd been fascinated by bees since childhood and

that, in all his years, he'd learned their great secret.

'What *is* their secret?' I asked, shading a hand over my eyes.

The farmer tugged the rough straw hat from his head, nudged a hand back through a crop of white hair, and replied:

'The secret of the bees is that, far from this quiet meadow, there lies an apian nirvana, where bees live as gods.'

My young eyes widened with awe at the thought of such a thing.

'Where is it — the nirvana?'

'Across the mountains, beyond the seas, and over the deserts.'

'Have you been there?'

The wizened stranger balked at the question.

'A man as humble as I has no hope of ever reaching the realm where bees are gods,' he said.

Standing tall, I pushed back my shoulders and whispered:

'Do you think *I* have a chance at locating the apian nirvana?'

The farmer drew a sharp fingernail down his cheek.

'You will find it only if you manage to gain the confidence of the bees.'

'You mean these bees here?'

'No, no... *all* of them.'

I didn't understand. How was I supposed to gain the confidence of all bees, everywhere?

Before I could give voice to the question, the old farmer wagged a finger in my direction.

'If the bees wish for you to find their sacred place, they will take you there,' he said.

And so it was that I took to the road, to search not for my fame and fortune, but for the mysterious apian nirvana of which the stranger had spoken.

I crossed the mountains and then seas.

Lame, I hobbled through deserts.

I trudged back and forth through forests that were in themselves great dominions.

Then, one winter night I took shelter from a blizzard in a yurt at the end of the world.

Crouching there, the wind howling outside, my bones shaking, I cursed myself for ever embarking on such a foolish quest.

Kindling a fire with the little dry wood, I gave thanks for the modest refuge.

As dense smoke and warmth filled the tent, I spied a pair of bees clinging to the canvas.

Cocking my ear towards them, I made out their conversation:

'We would be dead if that human hadn't lit the fire and opened a jar of honey for us,' the first bee said.

'He must have seen us freezing here and taken pity on us,' the second replied.

'Do you think he's going to the apian nirvana as well?'

'Of course he is — otherwise why would he be up here on the mountainside at the end of the world?'

My back warming with adrenalin and my mouth dry from expectation, I came to learn that the pair of bees would be setting out at first light for the place where their kind were worshipped as gods.

At first light, the bees stretched the muscles of their wings, calmed their breathing, and began the flight through the forest to the apian nirvana.

Hurrying after them, I managed to keep up, even though the snow was deep and the air ice-cold.

After hours of rushing through foliage at breakneck speed, the two bees vanished into a cleft in the ground. Uncertain whether I would fit, I forced myself through the narrow aperture.

To my amazement, I realized that I was inside a tunnel. Illuminated by shafts of natural light, its walls were lined with ancient hieroglyphs.

Anxious at being discovered and then punished for my intrusion, I kept as quiet as I could manage.

At the far end of the tunnel, I spied what appeared to be a great portal, the height of a hundred men.

Awed by such a spectacle, I hastened down the length of the tunnel, my gaze taking in hieroglyphic friezes festooned over either wall.

Approaching that great portal, I forced the immense doors open just wide enough to get inside.

On gaining entry, I was overcome by a sight from a tale worthy of Scheherazade herself.

Beyond the great portal was an immense chamber, hewn from the living rock.

All around, firebrands were flaring furiously, long shadows thrown over an altar fashioned in the shape of a honeybee.

Below it, moving as though they were dancing before a hive, were many hundreds of creatures. I use that word because, at first glance, it was uncertain from which species of life they hailed.

Drawing closer, I came to understand that they were in actual fact a strange fusion of bee and human. Although most were about my size, they bore wings, striped abdomens, and antennae.

Holding onto the wall for fear of collapsing from shock, my ears listened to the uproar of the secret rite.

To my amazement, I found that I could understand every word of it.

Fear giving way to unbridled fascination, I dropped down on my hands and knees and scurried closer to the edge of a natural gallery.

My eyes well-adjusted to the torch-light, I gazed in wonder at this, the apian nirvana.

As I did so, my breathing strained from excitement, I heard a voice in the language of the bees — spoken in reference to me:

'Alarm! Alarm! A trespasser is in our midst!'

Before I knew it, I had been captured, bound tight in twine.

Unable to move a muscle, I was marched to a hexagonal cell fashioned from reinforced wax.

Begging forgiveness, I pleaded for my freedom — exclaiming over and over that I was an admirer of bees.

Many hours passed.

Just as I was giving up hope, a guard appeared.

Like all the others, he was half-man, half-bee.

In the vernacular of the bees I questioned what was going on, but he didn't answer.

Instead, he escorted me through a hexagonal maze to an interrogation cell.

Waiting there was an officer.

Intrigued by what had led me to discover the secret sanctuary, he demanded to know how I had mastered the spoken language of the bees.

As I recounted the twists and turns of my tale, he listened.

When I was done with my story and drained of words, the official let out a shrill buzz, the likes of which I had not heard before.

A moment or two passed, then the wax floor on which I was standing grew warm and melted clean away.

Tumbling downwards, I found myself in a large hexagonal chamber.

An elderly member of the fraternity was standing there. Fearing he would attack me, I shielded my face.

But rather than mount an assault, he bowed down in reverence, his antennae quivering as though awed by my presence.

'Forgive our cruel welcome, O Wise One!' he buzzed. 'We have waited an eternity for your arrival!'

Perplexed at being welcomed as a respected guest, having been a prisoner only moments before, I expressed my gratitude.

'I don't understand how you knew I would be coming here,' I said.

Stepping over to a panel in the frieze, the ancient pointed to a scene surrounded by hieroglyphs.

'It is written,' he said.

'*Written*? What does it say?'

'In the Age of Distant Future, it is recorded that the Saviour of the Bees will come forth when least expected. Receive him with honour deserving of a deity and treat him as our ancestors decreed.'

Before I could pose another question, I was led to a sumptuous chamber. Adorned in fragrant flowers, the hexagonal quarters was as lovely a place as I have ever been.

Over the days that followed, a pretty young woman named Esel attended me. She fed me spoonfuls of the finest honey, rubbed the purest royal jelly into my skin, and sang songs of the bee ancestors.

'They always said you would come,' she whispered one night.

'Who did?'

'The elders.'

Peering into sweet Esel's eyes, I frowned.

'I don't understand what's happening,' I said. 'I am being hailed as though I were royalty, but at the same time I am a prisoner in this room.'

The maiden looked deep into my eyes, her expression strained.

'They revere you in a way that's fitting to your status.'

'What does that mean?'

Esel glanced away, as though unable to hold my stare.

'With time, you will know,' she answered.

As one day slipped into the next, I was fed more and more honey, and was lauded with every imaginable praise.

On the rare occasions that a member of the fraternity entered my quarters, they prostrated themselves on the wax floor, their wings trembling as though in the presence of a living god.

Whenever I asked if I could leave, my questions were met with alarm.

'Eat a little more honey, Your Excellence,' they would say, 'and forget

your troubles, because they no longer exist.'

Two weeks after arriving at the secret sanctuary, I implored Esel to be honest and to tell me all she knew. For the first time, I sensed her fear — not from speaking out, but rather from what was planned for me.

'There is to be a great celebration,' she said, her buzzing almost too soft to understand.

'What kind of celebration?'

'One that honours you.'

'Honours me? In what way?'

Esel's face froze.

'Mellification,' she said.

'*Mellification?*'

'It means a journey into the Afterlife, following an entombment in honey.'

By way of a secret passage, that sweet maiden showed me the Hall of the Ancients; the future — *my* future.

In a series of niches set along a stone wall were dozens of wax sarcophagi ornamented with hieroglyphs.

Esel explained how the caskets contained the mellified remains of the Ancestors.

'For a hundred days the Wise One is fed the finest honey, their skin bathed in royal jelly. Then, when the hexagonal bugle sounds, they are brought out from their quarters, worshipped, and...'

'*And?*'

'And, they are placed in a wax sarcophagus, their body steeped in honey.'

'They're going to kill me?' I buzzed, the words hollow and pained.

Esel lowered her head in a nod.

'You will be placed in a sarcophagus and kept in this niche, here.'

As I walked the length of the sacred wall, I noticed that some of the niches contained empty sarcophagi.

Before I could ask the reason, the maiden replied:

'In times of famine, one of the Ancestors is removed, and their body is eaten.'

'Why?'

'To give power to those of us left behind.'

Three days passed, in which I was unable to sleep.

My affection for honey and royal jelly extinguished, I sat on my bed and tried to think of a plan.

Sensitive to my predicament, Esel whispered:

'If you were to flee, they would hunt you and sting you to death.'

Another day slipped by.

Then, late one night, I made out a commotion in the sanctuary.

Peering out of my chamber, I saw hundreds of the bee brethren dressed in elaborate costumes.

'It's about to take place,' my kindly attendant said.

'What is?'

'The mellification. *Your* mellification.'

My heart pounding, I begged Esel to help me to escape.

'There is no escape,' she said, her buzz woeful and raw.

Just then, I made out the sound of feet marching down the corridor outside.

Before I knew it, I'd been scooped up and carried at shoulder height to a sarcophagus fashioned from the finest wax.

Hundreds of the brethren clustered around as the ceremonial casket was filled with boiling honey.

The elder stepped from the shadows.

'The Afterlife awaits you, O Wise One!' he exclaimed.

'Let me go! Let me return back through the forest!' I cried.

Against the backdrop of frantic excitement, my protest was useless.

Gripped tight by the arms, I was borne to the sarcophagus, the liquid honey boiling inside.

The elder raised a cane high above his head.

'As the Ancestors' bodies were preserved in honey, so the Wise One's will be!'

I cursed the elders, the brethren, and their guards.

Struggling, my lungs filled with the scent of bubbling honey.

As my shadow fell over that abominable sarcophagus, the shadow of another covered my own.

Esel.

In an act of selflessness greater than any other I have ever known, that beautiful young maiden threw herself into the casket.

Her young flesh boiling, she went without the faintest buzz of distress.

In the pandemonium that followed, I managed to make good my escape.

Hastening through the tunnels, the hieroglyphs observing my flight, I forced myself out from the slim aperture through which I had ventured.

To my surprise, the brethren did not hunt me.

Instead, I found myself in that forest at the end of the world, now charmed by spring.

I have no idea how long I stayed in the secret sanctuary.

What I do know is that I am alive today thanks to a maiden who gave her young life for my own.

It is to the memory of my beloved Esel that I have dedicated the remainder of my days.

As for honey, royal jelly, or the language of bees — they no longer feature in my life, save for in this wretched tale.

SKELETON ISLAND

Eight strangers were clustered
around the campfire
of the caravanserai —
silhouetted, ragged, and
ripened by adventure.
As the flames licked
the darkness, sparks
spitting up into the desert's
nocturnal firmament,
the traveller dressed in
indigo cleared his throat
and told his tale:

FIFTY SUMMERS AGO, when my skin was fresh and still scented with youth, I set sail from the eastern haunch of Arabia on the finest trading dhow ever to have kissed the waves.

Only the imagination of a child could picture the scene: dazzling sunlight mirrored off a seascape as mesmerizing a vision as any fantasy. Porpoises leaping to and fro; breakers cresting in the whitest white; the alluring stench of brine burning our nostrils.

Like me, the craft was young and spry, the sleek lines of her hull gliding so effortlessly towards the horizon that even the most hardened member of the crew proclaimed their awe. Our captain, a thickset crag of a man named Ibn Hamza, harnessed the breeze as I have never seen it harnessed since.

It was as though he understood the spoken language of the wind — not as a mortal but as the air itself. His hoarse voice spitting commands, he would give the order for the great lateen sail to be trimmed no more than a fraction of an inch.

In the hands of any other, that dhow would have been a packhorse, but with Ibn Hamza at the helm, she was a thoroughbred fit for a sultan's stables.

For six days and nights we followed a course eastward, a Damascene astrolabe and the stars revealing a route to beyond the next horizon.

At dusk on the seventh day, the captain called me to join him at the helm. Gesticulating at the Pole Star, he ordered me to keep it to the left of the sail.

'Our lives are in your hands,' he said through blistered lips. 'Fall asleep, and our graves will be down there.'

Ibn Hamza motioned to the blue-black swell, his eyes burning into mine. I promised not to relinquish my post and he vanished, leaving me alone.

All night I stood at the helm, the rounded curve of the wheel caressing my fingers, the Pole Star and the crescent moon glinting down seductively from the heavens. Never before had I felt so proud, or so excited by the prospect of adventure that lay ahead. I thought of my mother and my father wishing me a safe journey, of my brother making me promise to return before the year was out.

And I thought of the danger that, whether we liked it or not, was my shadow.

The more I weighed up the many perils, the more fearful I became. Huddled there in the darkness, with the lives of all in my own hands, I fretted whether I would ever survive the journey.

As I wondered and worried, a burning sensation seeded itself in the pit of my stomach.

As the ocean surged, the dhow lilted to the side — no more than a little at first. But, as I succumbed to the waves of fear, that glorious vessel heaved from port to starboard like a child's toy. Drawn into the approaching swell, the bow stooped low, then was jerked up high, the acacia timbers creaking so riotously that I feared they would split.

I cried out, but no one came to my aid. So, I yelled louder, my lungs half-filled with spray.

Still no answer.

Again, I thought of my parents, of my brother, and my sisters — each one tucked up safe in their beds without a care in the world.

I was about to utter a prayer when a voice called out above the tearing rage of wind.

'You imagine that you are on the deck of a vessel heading eastwards through turbulent seas.'

'Who's there?!'

The voice came again, deeper and more imperious than before:

'You may be young and foolish, but you are also blind!'

'Reveal yourself, O phantom!' I screamed. 'So that I may set eyes on our enemy!'

'It seems as though you have misunderstood not only the nature of your journey,' the voice replied, 'but friend from foe.'

'Who are you?!'

'Your saviour.'

'Saviour from *what*?!'

At that very instant, something took place that defied explanation.

As though unveiled by an eclipse, the crescent moon shone down with the force of a thousand suns.

Shading a hand to my eyes, I observed a wave rising up like a mountain on the surface of the sea.

So colossal was it that I could not move, speak, feel, or sense anything at

all. The only certainty was that, within moments, I would be dead, the proud young dhow smashed to splinters in the blink of a dazzled eye.

The great wave was so immense as to have the living presence of a mortal creature from the deep.

Ranging forwards across the last few yards of open water, it spoke:

'I am your saviour from *me*,' it said.

'Great wave! It is *you* that speaks?! Can you not simply surge to the side of our vessel?'

The great wave shuddered. As it did so, time seemed to slow to a halt.

'My course was charted centuries ago,' said the great wave.

'But why would you save me?'

The great wave shuddered once again, its monumental form the ultimate executioner.

'The young man standing there at the helm is destined to live a thousand lifetimes in one,' the voice whispered. 'In his journeys he will be known for his good deeds, but one in particular will be set apart from all the rest.'

As the great wave loomed up before me like a sentinel of death, I spat out the single question I could think of:

'Of what good deed do you speak?'

Holding back its waters, the wave shuddered yet again.

'You freed me,' it said.

'Freed *you*? How could I — a wretched speck of humanity — free a great wave as you?'

'I was imprisoned by a jinn,' the wave responded, its voice pained at the memory.

'But that's not possible!' I uttered, well aware that in the realm of the jinn, anything is possible.

'Are you not interested in when you save me, or where?'

I shook my head.

'I am far more interested to know how you plan to save me!'

The great wave let out a snort.

And in less time than it takes to tell, time was rolled forwards again, as it has since the dawn of creation.

The great wave tore through the water like a harbinger from hell.

A moment before it crushed the precious dhow into driftwood, drowning its proud captain and my fellow crew, I was cast into the sky.

Returned to its crescent form, the moon seemed to watch me as I shot upwards into the heavens, and then fell. And fell...

Even the poets of Persia could not describe the sense of that occult trajectory.

Twisting and turning through the tempest, the stars were up, and the black, brooding waters down.

Then the water was up, and the stars were down.

After tumbling for what seemed like an eternity, I came to a gentle rest on a beach, the waves lapping at the shore.

Having given effusive thanks to providence for my salvation, I clambered to my feet and took in my surroundings.

It seemed as though I was on a desert island, towering date palms and flourishing vegetation all around, streams and waterfalls, forests, and even caves for shelter. But there was, it seemed, no fauna.

Or, rather, at first glance I imagined there was not.

I have no idea at all quite how I knew, but something goaded me to close my eyes, to pause, to slow my thinking, and to look once again.

My sight recalibrated, I regarded the island a second time.

The horror! Rather than being devoid of fauna, the entire island was filled with it...

Men walking with their dogs, women clutching babes in arms, birds tweeting from the trees, and all manner of other creatures.

Creatures that were incomplete.

They were skeletons cheated of their flesh and sinew — sun-bleached bones as bright as the crescent moon had been.

Bewildered, I stood there on the beach, staring into the canopy of luxuriant undergrowth, watching the mesmerizing scene with incomprehension. How could it be? How could every living form be stripped of that which makes it corporeal?

A little time passed, and an ample-sized hound bounded up, sniffing the air as it came.

The animal's master followed, the miscellany of bones that were his feet imprinted in the sand.

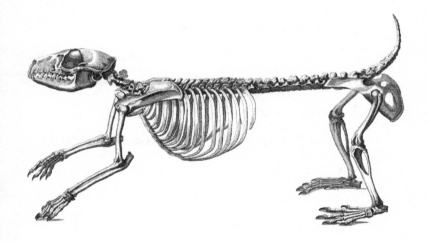

His skull raised high in anticipation, the animal's owner called a salutation in my own language.

Bewildered, I returned the greeting.

'What place is this?' was all I could think to ask.

'The island of Waq-Waq.'

The muscles of my face taut in a frown, I posed a second question:

'Are you dead?'

Calling his animal to heel, the skeleton leered at me in a smile.

'Why would you ask such a thing?'

'Because you have no flesh or muscle, no offal, heart, or brain.'

'Of course I don't,' the skeleton responded. 'Because I — or rather, *we* — we have progressed.'

'I don't understand,' I said.

Leading me into the undergrowth, the skeleton invited me to his village.

'Our ancestors were like you are,' he said as he walked. 'With elaborate biology, they were in need of constant food and were so often sick.

They needed sleep, clothing, not to mention soft furnishings in their homes. The animals of the island suffered in the same way.'

'So what happened to devolve you all?'

'*Devolve?*' the skeleton replied quizzically. 'You mean evolve — after all, we are superior. Look around you!'

And so I did. I spied skeleton children playing with bows and arrows in the village square, skeleton elders sitting in the shadows, skeleton chickens scratching at the dirt, and even skeleton monkeys tearing through the trees.

'We have none of the needs of your society,' the skeleton explained. 'We don't fight over possessions, food reserves, or land. We're not roasted by the summer sun, or worried by the monsoon downpour. We live in harmony.'

'What do you know about the world from which I come?' I asked.

The skeleton led me to a small enclosure made from sticks, as naked of foliage as he himself was naked of flesh.

'We have no need for food or clothing as you do,' he said, 'but we know all about the troubled lands of your world. On the dark nights when the east wind tears through the palm trees, our elders speak a ballad of a time when we were flesh on bones like you — preoccupied with the accessories of an empty life.'

Standing there in the village, skeletons hurrying hither and thither around me, I was struck that a frame of bones was preaching to me about fulfillment. As I turned the thought around in my mind, the skeleton said something that has haunted my waking hours and my dreams ever since:

'The ancient ballad that is both our history and our future records that a sailor will arrive on the shore when we least expect him to. His bones will be attired in flesh and skin, and he will be wearing clothing, such as our own ancestors wore. When he arrives, fresh-faced and proud, it is said that we must greet him with kindness and make the offering.'

'*Offering*? What offering?'

The skeleton that had found me down on the beach cocked his skull to the side, as if coaxing me gently to turn, which I did.

Clustered behind me was every man, woman, and child, every chicken, fox, rat, monkey, and bird from the island — each one a bundle of gleaming white bones.

His back crooked with age, an elder stepped forwards, a goblet held in outstretched hands.

'Our ancestors left this relic to us,' he said, his voice little more than a whisper. 'It is said that you are to drink the contents of the grail, so that you will be whole as we each are.'

'You will be whole,' the villagers echoed, the birds tweeted, and the dogs barked.

'You mean, I will become a skeleton just like you all?'

Every last skull dipped low in agreement.

'But... but... but I don't want to be like you,' I said.

The elder, in whose fleshless fingers the goblet was poised, sighed.

'Of course you do,' he avowed. 'Although you do not yet know it.'

Without another word, he stepped forwards, his old bones creaking as he came.

Behind him, the mass of bone forms grunted and groaned.

'You *must* drink,' the skeleton that had found me on the beach insisted.

'But why?'

'Because our antique ballad says so. And because, by drinking, harmony will be restored to the island of Waq-Waq.'

My mind racing, I struggled to think of how I might escape. I could have raced back to the shore, but what then? I had no craft awaiting me, and there was no great roc to clamber upon, as in the pages of *The Thousand Nights and a Night*.

And so, I did what many a sailor had done before, and has done since... I prayed...

Not to the heavens, or the Almighty.

Nor to the sun or the moon.

Or to the great wave that had borne me from the floundering vessel to the island of Waq-Waq.

Instead, I prayed to Sindbad.

I can hear you questioning the logic of my supplication. How, you are asking, could a character from the hallowed pages of an ancient treasury ever be expected to offer hope, when hope there most certainly was not?

And, of course, you are right to question, and even to scorn.

But, on the impenetrable dominion of what was Skeleton Island, where an antique ballad decreed what was done and what was not, it was the only hope.

My petition was borne on the breeze to the ears of Sindbad, sailor of seven voyages and seven seas.

No sooner had the final word left my lips, than a rumbling, grumbling sound swept over the hills, through the forest, and into the village where the grail was poised to my mouth.

As I watched in awe and consternation, a re-configuration occurred.

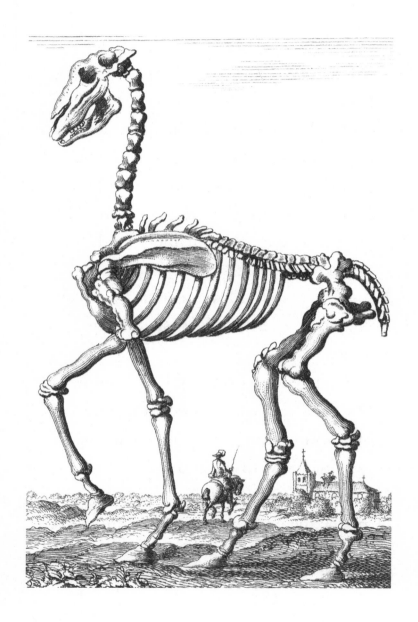

Every bone in every skeleton —
whether human or otherwise — came
loose.

One by one, and all at once, femurs
and jawbones, craniums, vertebrae, and
pelvic bones shot out in a tumultuous
frenzy of dazzling white... out from the
village of that abominable island, and
down to the beach.

Racing after it, I watched as the bones
constructed themselves silently into a
vessel.

Arranged by a sorcery known only to
Sindbad, the villagers and creatures of
Waq-Waq became the ship that was to
provide me with salvation.

After weaving sails from palm fronds
and taking on fresh water, fruit, and what
vegetables I could find growing in the

jungle, I set sail for my own land once again.

In all the years I have ventured across oceans and seas, never have I experienced a vessel equal to Sindbad's ship of salvation. Ripping through the water as though chased by the devil, she returned me to the eastern haunch of Arabia, whence I had come.

Thankful and bewildered, I stepped ashore.

Fashioned from the glinting, gleaming bones of Skeleton Island, that ghostly vessel trimmed her sails.

Then, setting off on the tide, she headed towards the distant horizon.

WELLSPRING

*Eight strangers were clustered
around the campfire
of the caravanserai —
silhouetted, ragged, and
ripened by adventure.
As the flames licked
the darkness, sparks
spitting up into the desert's
nocturnal firmament,
the traveller dressed in
indigo cleared his throat
and told his tale:*

For six generations my family have farmed a handful of fields on the leeward side of a barren mountain.

We keep sheep and goats, and grow enough in the way of vegetables for our own needs.

The land is rocky beyond compare, the climate harsh, and life one of hardship.

As a child, I remember my grandfather cursing his lot, wishing that our land was more fertile, and that the boulders and the rocks could be cleared.

Then, as an adolescent, I heard my father cursing the lot he had inherited.

Once it was my turn to take on the ancestral lands, I, too, moaned and groaned.

All the other farmers had fields without any rocks at all. It was as though an invisible force had picked up one corner

of the hillside and had given it a good shake — sending all boulders and rocks onto the land that it was my lot to work.

With such limited choices, we made less money than all the other farmers in the valley.

As a result, my wife, daughters, and myself had lived hand-to-mouth lives, beset with all manner of problems.

Our circumstances may not have been favourable, but the land of my ancestors awes me now as it has done since I was a child.

I always get up early enough to watch the sun break over the horizon — as my father, grandfather, and our ancestors must have done.

One morning, I was sitting on a great boulder right up at the top of the land, watching the darkness melt away.

The long sunrays streamed out, warming my face in the most joyous of sensations, gilding the landscape in a pristine sheet of gold.

For a moment I forgot all my troubles and woes.

Standing tall on that great rock, I surveyed the landscape and felt enormous pride.

As I glanced from one side of the valley to the other, I saw something glistening in the far corner of the farthest field.

On closer inspection, I realized it was a little spring of fresh water, which seemed to have only just broken through.

Cupping a little of the precious liquid in my hand, I raised it to my lips and drank.

Refreshing beyond words, it was absolutely delicious.

Taking one mouthful after the next, I took my fill, and immediately filled a bucket of the water and bore it down to the house for my family to enjoy.

That evening, when we sat down for dinner, I announced that I had a special pail of water. Scolding me for being so foolish, my wife said we were to find a suitor to marry our eldest daughter. Breaking down in tears at a tired subject being brought up once again, our eldest daughter fussed at not having all the books she wished for her studies.

Dinner was served, washed down with cups of the delicious water.

That night, I stretched out on the flat roof of our home, the canopy of stars glinting down at me. Falling into a deep sleep, I experienced a myriad of outlandish dreams.

Next evening, I mentioned the imaginings from the night before.

'I also experienced a frenzy of dreams,' said my wife.

'As did I,' intoned our eldest daughter.

'Perhaps it was the water,' I said.

My wife rolled her eyes.

'What nonsense!' she declared. 'We are having odd dreams because we live with so many problems.'

I frowned.

'The rocks and boulders are a blessing,' I said. 'I shall open a school for sculpture. The students will have all the stone they need, and the most wonderful landscape to inspire them.'

My wife frowned.

'We will find a husband for our eldest daughter,' she said, 'but not by searching for one. For, as everyone knows, appearing desperate is the root of our misfortune.'

Then our eldest daughter frowned.

'I shall borrow the books I need from our neighbour,' she said, 'and I shall repay her by darning the holes in all her blankets.'

'It was the water,' I said with certainty.

My wife and eldest daughter looked at me, as though clouds had been lifted from their minds.

'Yes it was,' they both said at once.

In the week that followed, I started a school for sculpture at the farm and began to make a fortune in the process. My wife ceased from her fretting about our eldest daughter and, in turn, she ceased from worrying about her studies. I even noticed that our cat, which had been lapping at the spring water too,

had worked out a way to trap and then devour all the mice in the house.

Before the second week was out, our eldest daughter was betrothed to a wealthy merchant from the neighbouring kingdom and was as content as she ever could be.

A little time passed, in which I put up a fence around the little spring, paid off my debts, and solved all the other problems that, until then, had beset my life.

Watching me keenly, the other farmers asked one another how I had ever managed to lift myself from poverty.

One evening, while sitting with a few friends in the teahouse, I declared that my success was down to the spring of most delicious water I'd discovered in the corner of my ancestral land.

What a fool I was to have spoken about it.

For, rather than lampoon me as I had expected them to do, the other farmers believed me.

Within a night and a day, every man, woman, and child from the village were in our field, awaiting their turn to drink from the spring.

Armed with every available pot, pan, and bucket, a line of people stretched all the way from the wellspring, down to village itself.

A day or two later, everyone who had drunk from that astonishing source had thought of solutions to the trials and tribulations of their lives.

All of a sudden, the villagers were walking tall and boasting of their good fortune.

There wasn't a question left in need of an answer, or a problem without a solution.

A week or so after the villagers had begun drinking from our spring, the thunder of hooves was heard charging in our direction.

Fearful that the neighbouring kingdom might invade, our king relied on a network of spies.

While listening out for enemy sympathizers, they had reported the recent goings on in our village.

Before I knew it, the royal guard seized me, along with an urn full of the prized water, and dragged me to the palace itself.

Within the hour, I was kneeling at the feet of the king, who was sitting imperiously on a great golden throne.

I have never seen a man as protected as our leader. Anxious beyond belief at being stabbed, beheaded, shot, or poisoned by his enemies, it seemed as though he had not slept for many weeks.

As soon as he saw me, he scowled with suspicion.

'I hear that you have located a source of magic water,' he boomed, 'but I believe it to be nothing but a cunning ploy to end my life!'

'Your Majesty,' I responded, 'I am a humble farmer, but the wellspring I discovered does indeed appear to give solutions to problems.'

'Our enemies are plotting to overthrow our kingdom,' the monarch said, his voice trembling. 'So, tell me what the solution is for that!'

'From our experimentation with the water,' I explained, 'it appears that the person wishing for an answer to their problem must ingest a little of the water directly. As it is not my head the enemies want on a pole, I cannot provide an answer to the problem at hand.'

'How do I know that you have not poisoned that water in the urn before you?' the king enquired.

'With respect, Your Majesty,' I said, 'it was not I who asked to come here. Rather, I was brought by your armed guards and threatened with imprisonment if I did not comply.'

'It could easily be part of a clever ruse!' the monarch grunted. 'As we well know, our enemies are experts in deception.'

'Drink a little of the liquid,' I said, 'and, Your Majesty, you shall have the answers you require.'

Grunting and growling, the king clicked his fingers.

A magnificent crystal glass was borne forwards on a silken cushion, and a little of the liquid was poured into it. The royal taster took a sip.

When he did not drop dead, the king touched the rim of the glass to his lips.

Almost at once, it was as though a light was turned on in the monarch's mind, and the clouds of cruel incompetence were lifted.

Staring into the middle distance, he grinned from ear to ear.

'Of course!' he exclaimed. 'I see it now, but I don't understand why I didn't see it before!'

A vizier, poised to the right of the throne, raised an eyebrow.

'See *it*, Your Majesty?'

'I see the answer to our dilemma — how to bring peace to the kingdom.'

As was common knowledge in both our kingdoms, our king, and that of the neighbouring one, were devoted to the game of chess.

Each one of them adored the game as much as they did life itself.

Using chess as a route to peace, the king saw to it that a new age of universal harmony began.

A little more time elapsed and, by royal decree, a pipe was laid from the wellspring to the palace.

Every single man, woman, and child in the kingdom was allowed a ration of the

water on the condition that they swore unfailing allegiance to the king.

As the weeks and months passed, I came to notice a change in the kingdom.

No longer troubled by difficulties, with no need to work out answers for themselves, the populace slipped into a state of apathy.

No one ever squabbled, argued, or ever got jealous of one another.

By consuming their ration of the water each week, everyone instantly had the answers they needed.

The situation may sound blissful to your ears, but believe me, it was not.

Without pressing concerns to rally them through their lives, the people grew disillusioned and sad.

They had answers to every possible dilemma, but not even the water from my ancestral spring could provide an antidote to that.

One evening, I went up into the field with a hammer and a spade.

All night I toiled, breaking one of the boulders into gravel. When I had a good amount, I carried it over to the spring. And, digging the area out as best I could, I filled it with the gravel. After that, I laid down topsoil, so that it looked as though the spring had never been there at all.

The next day, the guard arrived from the palace and demanded to be told why the spring was no longer sending water to the town.

'It dried up as unexpectedly as it appeared,' I said.

The news was passed from mouth to ear, until every man, woman, and child in the kingdom had learned the news.

At first they all seemed sadder than sad.

Some people tore out their hair and questioned how they would ever survive without the problem-solving water.

Others muttered, spluttered, moaned and groaned, blaming the spring drying up on the neighbouring kingdom.

A week or two of withdrawal symptoms came and went.

But then, everything went back to normal.

In the palace, the king was as mistrustful as ever once again.

In village squares, farmyards, teahouses, and homes, people bickered and whined, anxious because of their problems — as people have bickered and whined since the beginning of the world.

As for me, I set off on a journey —
a journey encumbered by a flood of
delicious problems.

Crossing a hundred horizons,
and a hundred more, I reached this
caravanserai on this fair night.

And that, my friends, is the tale I have
to tell.

Finis

A REQUEST

If you enjoyed this book, please review it on your favourite online retailer or review website.

Reviews are an author's best friend.

To stay in touch with Tahir Shah, and to hear about his upcoming releases before anyone else, please sign up for his mailing list:

 http://tahirshah.com/newsletter

And to follow him on social media, please go to any of the following links:

http://www.twitter.com/humanstew

@tahirshah999

http://www.facebook.com/TahirShahAuthor

http://www.youtube.com/user/tahirshah999

http://www.pinterest.com/tahirshah

https://www.goodreads.com/tahirshahauthor

http://www.tahirshah.com

Made in the USA
Las Vegas, NV
08 January 2022

40810280R00152